MACY IS C

by Michèle Dufresne

Pioneer Valley Educational Press, Inc.

One afternoon, Mom and Alex and Derek went to the park. Macy the dog went with them.

Mom sat down on the park bench. "I'm going to sit here and do some work," she told the boys.

"Hey! Let's play soccer," said Derek.

Alex and Derek started to kick the soccer ball up and down the field.

Then Alex kicked the ball so hard that it went into the woods.

Alex and Derek ran into the woods to get the ball.

"I've got it," said Derek.

"Hey! Look at the path," said Alex. "Let's follow it and see where it goes." The two boys walked down the path. Soon they were far into the woods.

Mom looked up from her work.
She could not see the boys.
"Macy, where are the boys?"
she asked.

"Woof!" said Macy.

Macy ran to the woods.
"Are they in the woods?"
Mom asked.

"Woof!" said Macy.
Macy ran down the path.

Mom followed Macy.
They walked and walked.
"Alex! Derek!" called Mom.
"Where are you?"

Alex and Derek came running out of the woods. "We're glad you found us," said Derek. "We couldn't find our way back!"

"I didn't find you," said Mom. "It was Macy! Macy, you are a clever dog!"